THE BIG BOOK OF

Mind-
Stretchers

CW01095416

Other books by Gyles Brandreth

All published by Corgi Books

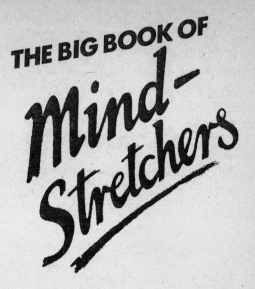

THE BIG BOOK OF
Mind-Stretchers

Gyles Brandreth

Illustrated by David Simonds

CORGI BOOKS
A DIVISION OF TRANSWORLD PUBLISHERS
LTD.

THE BIG BOOK OF MINDSTRETCHERS

A CORGI BOOK 0 552 54272 5

First published in Great Britain in 1986 by Corgi Books

Corgi edition published 1986

Corgi Books are published by Transworld Publishers Ltd.,
61 – 63 Uxbridge Road, Ealing, London W5 5SA.

Made and printed in Great Britain by
Cox & Wyman Ltd., Reading, Berks.

INTRODUCTION

How good are you at solving problems?

Can you make eight 8s equal 1000, work out what on earth IME means, or tell how many 7s there are in seven hundred and seven million, seven hundred and seventy-seven thousand, seven hundred and seven?

Baffled? Or did you find it all very easy? Either way you will find lots to amuse you in this book: it contains one hundred brain-boggling puzzles. There are number puzzles and word puzzles, picture puzzles and riddles, optical illusions, matchstick puzzles and logic puzzles of all shapes and sizes. Some are easier than they seem (though a few are more difficult), but all are tantalising and great fun to do.

Are you equal to the challenge? Then sharpen up your wits, find a pencil and paper to help you work out the solutions, and see how many you can solve. And if you get really stuck, don't despair, the answers are at the back!

Eyles

1: THE GREAT EASTER EGG HUNT

It was Easter Sunday, and the Great Easter Egg Hunt was on! To find her Easter egg, all Emma had to do was take the correct ribbon out of the basket.

"It's not next to the brown ribbon," said her mother.

"Mine's the orange one," said her sister Sally.

Her brother Richard also had a piece of advice, *"My ribbon isn't blue."*

Her cousin Alison told her, *"My ribbon is next to Richard's."*

Finally her father added, *"Emma, your ribbon is further from Richard's than Sally's."*

If you were Emma, which ribbon would you choose?

2: A WEATHER FORECAST

Young Jack Frost had always fancied himself as a bit of an amateur weather forecaster. Once, in the middle of the night, he woke up to find that it was pouring with rain. This surprised him because it was summer at the time. However, he confidently predicted that in seventy-two hours' time, there would still be no sign of sunny weather. How could he be so sure?

3: YARDSTICKS

If I gave you thirteen matches, each measuring two inches, and asked you to put them together to make one yard, you would probably think I was crazy. Maybe I am — but there is a way of doing it! Do you know what it is?

4: SILLY PHILLY

One day, Philly Phillipson received an urgent telephone call from her father. He told her that he had to go on a business trip the following day, and would need some new clothes. He asked her if she would do some shopping for him. Philly's father always kept some spare money in an envelope at the back of his wardrobe, and she found the envelope with the number 98 written on it in red felt pen.

Philly bought her father £90 worth of clothes thinking that she would have money to spare, but when she looked inside the envelope at the cash desk, she was embarrassed to discover that she did not have enough. Can you explain silly Philly's mistake?

5: DON'T COUNT YOUR EGGS . . .

One morning, Farmer McDonald woke up to discover that his hen had laid five huge brown eggs during the night. He placed all five eggs in a basket and decided to share them among his five daughters. Each was given an egg, but one egg remained in the farmer's basket. Can you work out what the farmer did?

6: SPOT THE FORGERY

There are ten stacks of ten-pence pieces standing on a table, each stack consisting of ten coins. One whole stack is made up of forgeries, but you do not know which one. What you **do** know is that a genuine ten-pence piece weighs 10 grams, and that a forgery weighs one gram more. Using a scale and some gram weights, what is the smallest number of weighings you would need to find out which stack contains the forgeries?

7: TOO EASY?

Can you think of a common English word which ends in ENY? Or how about another common word ending in the letters MT? It's not as easy as it seems, is it?

8: SUPER SUNFLOWER

There is a sunflower in my garden which has been growing at a very fast rate. For the past sixteen weeks, it has doubled its height every week, until it's now a staggering 480 cm high. Can you work out how many weeks it took my super sunflower to reach 240 cm?

9: ALL THE SEVENS

How many sevens are there in the figure seven hundred and seven million, seven hundred and seventy-seven thousand, seven hundred and seven?

10: FOUR BALLS

If you had four balls like the ones pictured below, could you arrange them so that **each** one was touching **all** the other three?

11: SCATTY CATS

Mrs Kitty Purrs was a great animal lover and particularly fond of cats. Her house was always full of all sorts of stray and lonely pussies. For example, in one rather small room a cat was sitting in each of the four corners, and opposite each of these cats, three cats were sitting, and by each cat's tail a cat was sitting. Can you work out the total number of cats Kitty had in this small room?

12: ROMAN MATCHES

Borrow a matchbox from somebody and use twelve matches to make the sum shown below. The Roman numerals show that 6 — 4 = 9, and you don't have to wear a toga to know that something is wrong with that sum! Can you make the sum make sense by moving **just one** match?

13: WATER, WATER

Imagine you are sunbathing on the deck of a yacht just off the Costa Mucha in the Mediterranean. There is a rope ladder hanging over the side of the boat, and it has ten rungs. The distance between each rung is 40 centimetres, and the lowest rung is just touching the surface of the water. Because of the incoming tide, the water is rising at a rate of 10 centimetres an hour. How soon will the surface of the water cover the fourth rung from the top of the rope ladder?

14: ROGER THE DODGER

Little Roger Rascal came rushing in from the garden one day with a smile all over his face. "Mum, mum," he shouted, "I've just found an ancient coin buried at the far end of the garden — it must be worth thousands of pounds." Mrs Rascal was used to her son's elaborate hoaxes but she decided to listen to Roger's story just in case it was true. It was only when he told her that the coin was dated 55 BC that she knew for sure that he was up to his old tricks.

How did Mrs Rascal know that it was impossible for Roger to find a coin dated 55 BC ?

15: A MEETING OF OPPOSITES

Edgar and Edmund O'Leary were twin brothers, but one lived in Bristol and the other in London. One day they both had exactly the same idea, as twins often do — they decided to visit each other. So Edgar left Bristol at noon in his brand-new sports car, while Edmund set off from London at exactly the same time, but at a rather slower pace, on his bicycle.

When Edgar and Edmund met on the road from Bristol to London, which of the twins was nearer London?

16: UPSIDE-DOWN YEAR

Can you think of the last year which would look the same upside-down as right-side up? (Here's a clue — one such year, though not the last one, is 1881.)

17: HOW OLD AM I?

When my mother was 29, I was only 6. Now she is exactly twice as old as I am. How old am I now?

18: PRICEY BOOK

Professor Albert Schickelgroober, a well-known mathematician, went into his local bookshop one afternoon. The shop assistant decided to give him a little maths test of his own. He told the Professor that the book cost £1 plus half its price. After a few moments Professor Schickelgroober began to smile, and handed the assistant the correct money. How much did he pay for the book?

19: AS GOOD AS GOLD

When the bank-robber eventually broke into the vault, he found two piles of gold bars and a pair of scales. The first consisted of £100 bars, and the second pile was made up of £200 bars. If the first pile weighed 100 kilos and the second pile weighed 50 kilos, which pile was worth more to the robber?

20: TWO'S COMPANY, THREE'S A CROWD

A farmer has to take a wolf, a hen, and some corn across a river. The problem is that his rowing boat is only big enough to hold the farmer plus **either** the wolf **or** the hen **or** the corn. He knows that if he takes the corn with him, the wolf will eat the hen, and if he takes the wolf with him, the hen will eat the corn. Only when the farmer himself is present are the hen the corn safe from their enemies. In spite of all these difficulties, the farmer manages to take all three across the river. How on earth does he do it?

21: ONE ACROSS

How about this for a strange crossword clue:

1. H I J K L M N O

Think about it — the answer is something we come into contact with all the time.

22: BROTHERS AND SISTERS

Mr and Mrs Large and their family lived in a big house in the country. Each of their sons had as many sisters as brothers, but each of their daughters had only half as many sisters as brothers. How many brothers and sisters are there in the large Large family?

23: PIECES OF EIGHT

Using only plus signs, you can make five 2s make 28. Here's how: 22 + 2 + 2 + 2 = 28.

Now, can you do the same sort of thing with eight 8s, and make 1000?

24: A CENTURY

There are lots of ways to make one hundred, but can you think of a way of doing it with five 1s, using either a plus sign or a minus sign?

25: BOARDGAME

Have a look at this chessboard.

It consists of 32 black squares and 32 white squares, but can you count up the total number of **'black and white'** squares on the board? (Here's a clue: the squares can be of any size!)

26: CRAZY FRACTIONS

I'm looking for a number. All I can say is that a half is a third of it. Can you see through this fraction gobbledygook and find the answer?

27: SHAPES AND NUMBERS

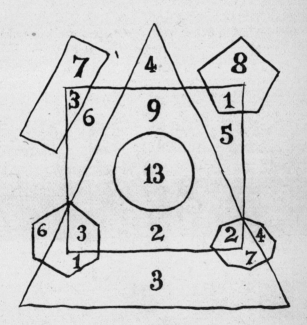

What is the sum of the figures:

a. In the square?

b. In the hexagon and octagon, but not in the square?

c. In the triangle, but not in the circle?

d. In the rectangle and hexagon, but not in the triangle?

e. In the triangle and pentagon?

28: GET AN EARFUL

In the village of Amazonia in the South American jungle, there live 400 women. Five per cent of them wear just one earring. Of the remaining ninety-five per cent, half wear two earrings and half do not wear any earrings at all. What is the total number of earrings worn by the women of Amazonia?

29: EGG ON THE FACE

Which of these two sentences is correct?

1. The yolks of eggs are white.
2. The yolks of eggs is white.

30: THE CHURCH CLOCK

If the church clock in Lower Woppingham takes five seconds to strike six, how long does it take to strike twelve?

31: HAZEL'S HAD IT

The following sentence contains a staggering NINE 'had's in a row:

Joan where Hazel had had had had had had had had had the teacher's approval.

Though it may seem difficult to believe, there is a way of punctuating this sentence so that it makes sense.

32: IN THE LABORATORY

Professor Bunsen was working late in the lab one night, trying to perfect a very important experiment. He discovered that when he wore his hat, the experiment took 80 minutes, and when he didn't wear his

hat, the same experiment took one hour and 20 minutes. How do you account for these strange goings on?

33: WAITER, WAITER

A woman in a restaurant was horrified to discover a dead fly floating in her coffee. She immediately hailed a waiter, and asked him to fetch her a completely fresh cup of coffee. After taking one sip of the cup the waiter brought her, the woman exclaimed, *"How dare you! I'm certain this is the same cup of coffee I had before, only with the fly removed."* How could the woman be so sure?

34: EXOTIC ANIMALS

When five animal crates arrived at Greystoke Zoo with their name tags all mixed up, the zoo keeper was very puzzled. Can you help him to unscramble the more common names for these truly 'exotic' beasts?

1. THE PANEL
2. ALL GOT AIR
3. RELENT A TASK
4. AUNT GROAN
5. AWFUL FAT BORE

35: FISH AND CHIPS

One day, Harry Haddock thought it was about time to get a new sign put up outside his fish shop. When the sign-painter had finished the job, the new sign looked something like this:

Harry was not pleased, and said something to the sign-painter which was not only a completely grammatical sentence, but which contained five 'and's in a row. Do you know what Harry Haddock said?

36: MONEY PROBLEMS

If the correct way to write nine thousand nine hundred and nine pounds is £9,909 — and, of course, it is — what is the correct way of writing twelve thousand twelve hundred and twelve pounds?

37: A TALKING PARROT

Johnny Silver wanted to buy his mother a talking parrot for her birthday. The pet shop salesman pointed to a brightly-coloured parrot saying, *"I guarantee that this parrot will repeat every word it hears."* Johnny was delighted with this news, and immediately bought the parrot for his mother.

Johnny and his mother soon discovered that the parrot would not speak a single word, and yet the salesman had told the truth. Can you explain?

38: IT'S NOTHING

What is **1** multiplied by **2**
multiplied by **3**
multiplied by **4**
multiplied by **5**
multiplied by **6**
multiplied by **7**
multiplied by **8**
multiplied by **9**
multiplied by **0**?

Can you see the sting in the tail of this mindstretcher?

39: THREE ERRORS

This mindstretcher contains three mistakes. What are they?

a. $2 + 2 = 4$
b. $4 \div \frac{1}{4} = 4$
c. $5\frac{1}{2} \div \frac{1}{2} = 11$
d. $6 - (-3) = 3$
e. $9 \times \frac{2}{3} = 6$

40: CHOICE OF CUTS

One day, a cowboy rode into a small town in Arizona. He had been on the trail for many weeks, and decided he needed a haircut. The town only had two barbers, each with his own shop. The cowboy had a look inside the first shop, and saw that it was spick and span. The barber was freshly shaved, immaculately dressed, his hair neatly trimmed. The other shop looked as if a bomb had hit it. The barber was dirty and shabby, his hair a complete mess. After a few moments' thought, the cowboy chose the second barber to cut his hair. Why?

41: AN APPLE IN THE HAND . . .

If you took five apples from a basket that contained fifteen apples, how many apples would you have?

42: FOUR LETTERS

Imagine you have written four letters to four different people, and have addressed four envelopes. If you put the letters into the envelopes **at random**, what is the likelihood that exactly three letters will go into the right envelopes?

43: RAT TRAP

If five cats can kill five rats in only five minutes, how long will it take 555 cats to kill 555 rats?

44: WATCH IT

Mr Tick and Mr Tock both have a little trouble with their watches. Mr Tick's watch gains one minute every hour, while Mr Tock's watch loses one minute every hour. If they both set their watches to the correct time at 6 p.m. on Friday night, when will there be a difference of exactly one hour in the times shown by their two watches?

45: TOPSY-TURVY

Some three-figure numbers can do things that other three-figure numbers can't! I have found one which, when it is turned upside down and subtracted from itself, leaves the answer 303. Do you know what it is?

46: STRANGE MESSAGES

Do you know what this means? It is something you learn at school: **ie cXCEPT**. It's a way of writing *'I before E except after C'* ! Here are some more well-known phrases which have been made into strange messages.

a. CCCCCCC

b. $\frac{\text{Stand U}}{\text{I}}$

c. IME

d. $\frac{\text{Girl}}{\text{Slept}}$

e. 6pmin5pm

47: A REAL WINDFALL

One Christmas, Len and Lesley Lloyd received news of a great windfall — they were each left £1000 by their Great-aunt Grizelda. During the next year, neither Len nor Lesley stole a penny, and yet by the following Christmas they had over £50,000 between them! Have you any idea how they did it?

48: THE LT CLUB

My attention has been brought to the existence of a most extraordinary club, called the LT Club. Every member is either a 'liar', who always lies, or a 'truther', who always tells the truth. When I visited the club recently, I found its members seated around a huge circular table. It was impossible to tell simply by looking at them which was a 'liar' and which a 'truther', so I asked each man in turn which of the two he was. They all assured me they were 'truthers'. The 'truthers' were telling the truth, and the 'liars' were lying! I tried a different approach, this time asking each man whether the person on his left was a 'truther' or a 'liar'. This time each one told me that the man on his left was a 'liar'.

While thinking about the LT Club later that night, I realised that I had not counted the number of men at the table, so I telephoned the club's President. He told me there were 35 present. After I had put the phone down, it occurred to me that I could not rely on this figure because I did not know if the President was a 'truther' or a 'liar'! When I telephoned the club's Secretary, he told me that the President was a 'liar', and that there were actually 40 men present at the table.

Which man, if either, should I have believed, on the basis of what I saw that day?

49: THE MISSING POUND

Freddy Franklin, a travelling salesman of many years' experience, booked a room for the night at the Astoria Hotel. He paid the hotel clerk £20, and went upstairs. When the clerk realised that he had overcharged for the room by £5, he sent a bellboy up to see Freddy with five £1 notes. The dishonest bellboy gave three to Freddy, keeping the other two for himself.

Freddy has now paid £17 altogether for the room, and the bellboy has made £2. That accounts for £19. Where is the missing pound?

50: THE COCKTAIL CHERRY

Place four matches in the pattern shown below to form a cocktail glass, with a small coin acting as the cocktail cherry.

Can you now move two matches (and **only** two) to new positions so that the cherry is outside the glass, and the glass is reformed in a different position? Remember, the glass must not change its size or shape.

51: A BIG HOLE

Eric has just dug a hole that is 36 cm deep, 23 cm wide, 32cm long. What is the volume of earth in the hole?

52: KNOCK KNOCK

Knock! Knock!
Who's there?
Bob.
Bob who?
Bobsleigh!

The answers to the following clues all begin with boys'
or girls' names. So, Knock! Knock! . . . . . . Who's
there!

a.	TOM	(A Drum)
b.	BEN	(Under)
c.	JACK	(The big prize)
d.	PAT	(Touching)
e.	MARK	(Saleable)
f.	PHIL	(A Wise Thinker)
g.	LEO	(A Spotted Animal)

53: AN ANCIENT PROBLEM

Romulus Remus was born in Rome in 36 BC. He led a happy life, and lived to quite an old age. Exactly how old was he on his birthday in AD 38?

54: STRANGE CHANGE

Johnny Bell was asked to go to the shops by his mother one day. She gave him £5, and when he returned he gave her back the change. He placed in her hand two coins totalling 55 pence, but one of the coins was not a 50-pence piece. What two coins did Johnny give his mother?

55: LIKE FATHER, LIKE SON

Two fathers and two sons went into a café to have something to eat. The bill came to £3, and they all spent the same amount. How much did each of them spend?

56: THE DUD NOTE

A man walked into a sweet shop and bought a box of chocolates costing £3. He paid with a £5-note, which the shopkeeper could not change, so he had to go next door to the tobacconist, who was able to give the shopkeeper five £1 coins in exchange. The customer was given his £2, and he then left.

The next day, the tobacconist walked into the shop and told the shopkeeper that the £5-note was a forgery. The owner of the shop had no option but to give him his £5 back. How much did the owner of the sweet shop lose altogether?

57: THE DONKEY AND THE MULE

A mule and a donkey were walking down the road, struggling with a load of sacks on their backs. The donkey was groaning loudly, so the mule turned to him and said: *"Why are you complaining? If you gave me one of your sacks, I would have twice as many as you, but if I gave you one of my sacks, then we would be carrying equal loads."* How many sacks did each have?

58: A PIPE DREAM

The pipe-layer in this village has got a problem. A pipe has to be laid from the gasworks, the waterworks, and the power station to each of the three neighbouring houses. There is one small snag — the pipes must not cross each other. Can you solve the pipe-layer's problem by pencilling in a suitable route for the pipes?

59: AN ANCIENT RIDDLE

When the famous Greek mathematician Diophantes
died, the following riddle was carved on his grave:

> *"This stone marks the grave of Diophantes.*
> *If you solve this riddle, you will know his age.*
> *He spent one-sixth of his life as a child,*
> *Then one-twelfth as a youth.*
> *He was married for one-seventh of his life.*
> *Five years after he married, his son was born.*
> *Fate overtook his beloved child; he died*
> *When he was half the age of his father.*
> *Four more years did the father live*
> *Before reaching the end of his life."*

Can you work out how long Diophantes lived?

60: THE WAY THE WIND BLOWS

If an electric train is travelling northwards at a steady
60 kph, and the wind is blowing due south at a rate of
55 kph, in which direction is the smoke pointing?

61: AN ARABIAN TALE

The following mindstretcher was first thought of by the
peoples of Ancient Arabia, where the piastre was the
normal currency.

A hunter was hunting alone and was starting to run
very short of food. By chance, he ran into two shepherds, one of whom had three small loaves and the
other five. When the hunter asked them for some of
their food, they kindly agreed to divide the loaves
equally among the three of them. The hunter thanked
them heartily for the food, and paid them eight
piastres. How should the shepherds divide the money?

I'd advise you to take your time about this one,
because mindstretchers don't last thousands of years
without good reason!

62: HEART TO HEART

Do you know what this is?

63: FILL THE GAPS

Can you supply the missing numbers in these series?

a. 1 1 2 3 – 8 13 –
b. 7 8 5 6 – 4 1 –
c. 6 8 24 32 96 128 – –
d. 3 3 5 4 4 3 5 –
e. 8 9 7 8 9 6 –

64: ON THE BOIL

If it takes three and a half minutes to boil an egg, how long does it take to boil four eggs?

65: BREAK THE CODE

Believe it or not these numbers form a coded message.
Break the code and the secret message is yours!

3 15 4 5   2 18 5 1 11 5 18 19   15 6   20 8 5
23 15 18 12 4   21 14 9 20 5

66: BLACK AND WHITE

I have a sealed box which contains two balls. All that is known about the balls is that one is black and one is white. Is there any way I can find out their colours without taking them out of the box?

67: MISSING BOYS

Each of these words has a number of letters missing. The funny thing is that each group of missing letters is a boy's name!

1. P – I S T
2. A – I C
3. C L – A L
4. B – C E
5. C A – D A R
6. S – U L A N T
7. B E T – A L
8. S – E T
9. – B A
10. – A L T Y

68: CROSSWORD PUZZLE

Can you solve this crossword puzzle with the help of these clues:

ACROSS

1. Found in a pod.
2. Is in debt.
3. Prince Charles has two.
4. Afternoon meals.

DOWN

1. The left side of a ship.
2. A harbour.
3. Fortified wine.
4. A gate.

69: A TIGHT SQUEEZE

One morning Bobby Bell found a 6-metre-long hollow iron pipe. He measured the width of the mouth of the pipe, and found it was 8 centimetres. It was the same width both ends, and it looked the same width all the way along its length. Bobby decided to try a little experiment. He wanted to see if it was possible to put a steel ball measuring 6 centimetres across in one end, and a similar ball measuring 4 centimetres across in the other end, and get them both to emerge at their opposite ends. Do you think it is possible?

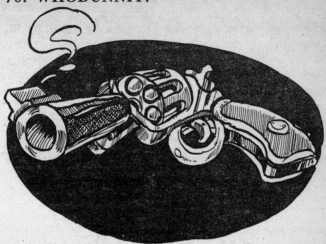

One month ago, five men were sitting together in a café. They were in the middle of a fierce argument when one of them suddenly pulled a gun from his pocket and shot dead one of the others. The four remaining men were taken to the local police station that same day, where they made the following statements, all of which are true:

JOHN: Last week, Paul had a game of rugby with one of the innocent men.

TIM: The murderer is my flat-mate — we've known each other for years.

ALAN: The murderer went into hospital only two weeks ago with a broken leg.

PAUL: Alan and Tim aren't exactly friends — they met for the first time today in the café.

WHODUNNIT?

71: TRYING TRIANGLE!

How many triangles (of any size) can you find in this diagram?

72: NONSENSE MAKES SENSE

Can you make any sense of this?

I SNOTEA   NLET TERSSL   LID
T   SYWHE   IPANDS   E

73: THE L-SHAPE

Can you divide this L-shape into four parts of equal size and shape?

74: AN ODD SUM

Using eight matches, can you prove that half of twelve is seven? Here's clue — it's more Roman than Arabic!

75: SPEEDING ALONG

Benny Brown set off from London in his brand-new car to visit some friends in Wales. His average speed for the whole journey was 60 kph, and he arrived an hour earlier than he would have done if his average speed had been 50 kph. Can you work out the total distance Benny Brown travelled?

76: FRONT AND BACK

- E R G R O -

The same three letters can be placed before and after these five letters to form a common eleven-letter word. What is that word?

77: THE ENVELOPE TEST

Try to draw this envelope in **one continuous line**, without crossing a line, retracing a line, or lifting your pencil off the paper.

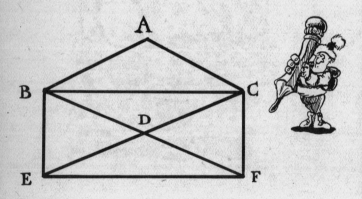

78: THE TRIANGLE TEST

Keeping in mind the same restrictions as above, draw these triangles in **one continuous line**.

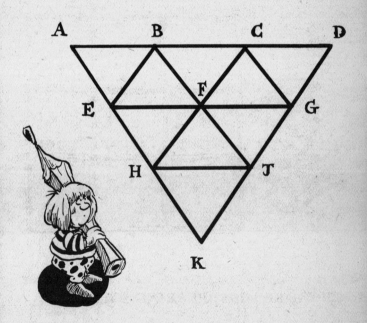

79: DISAPPEARING SQUARES

Using 24 matches, construct the shape below.

Now, by removing 8 matches, leave just two squares visible.

80: MORE DISAPPEARING SQUARES

Starting with the same original shape, remove four matches, and leave five squares visible.

81: ALL THE NATIONS

All the clues relate to words which end in the word
-nation. What *-nation*:

1. Is the most hated?
2. Is a murder?
3. Is a kind of acting?
4. Is dreaded by schoolchildren?
5. Brings light?
6. Is a flower?
7. Enchants you?
8. Is the final goal?
9. Is the ability to make things up?
10. Is the end?

82: A SPECIAL NUMBER

I am after a very special number. If this number is multiplied by 1000, the answer is **less** than if the same number is added to 1000. Do you know what it is?

83: WHAT AGE?

I am looking for words which end in *-age*. Can you work out what I want using these clues?

1. What is a butcher's -age?
2. What is a rugby player's -age?
3. What is an electrician's -age?
4. What is a letter's -age?
5. What is a traveller's -age?
6. What is a drink's -age?
7. What is a bird's -age?

Which of these two lines is longer — the horizontal or the vertical?

85: PLAYING CARDS

There are three playing cards placed in a row on a table. From these four clues, can you work out the number and suit of each card?

1. A diamond is on the left of a spade (not necessarily right next to it).
2. An eight is on the right of a king.
3. A ten is on the left of a heart.
4. A heart is on the left of a spade.

86: JEREMIAH'S CHOICE

Jeremiah Jackson had been a trapper in the Rocky Mountains all his life. One winter, he was delayed out in the open by a freak snowstorm, and, by the time he reached his log cabin, he was freezing and frost-bitten! When he finally opened the door of the cabin, he was confronted with a choice of what to do next. He looked at the fireplace full of wood; he looked at the candle by his bed; he looked at the full oil-lamp dangling from the ceiling; and finally he looked at the match in his icy hand — it was his last one. Hovering on the brink of death by freezing, Jeremiah had to make a quick decision on which to light first. What would you have done?

87: EACH TO THEIR OWN

If I told you that jewellers only ate carrots (carats), could you tell me what these people might eat?

a. AN ACTOR   e. A PLUMBER
b. AN ELECTRICIAN   f. A SHOE-MAKER
c. A FOOT-DOCTOR   g. A GAMBLER
d. A TRAFFIC WARDEN   h. A CASTAWAY

88: RINGS BEFORE THE EYES

Have a look at these four circles, and tell me whether you think the distance between A and B is greater or less than the distance between C and D — without using a ruler, of course!

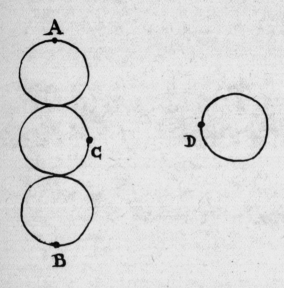

89: ONE SMALL STEP

From old words, new words can be made! Add one letter to the following words, jumble them up, and, using the clues as a help, come up with a totally new word.

1. LINES (Quiet)
2. ACHE (Shore)
3. BRUTE (Servant)
4. MUCH (Pals)
5. PANEL (Mars)
6. THIS (Garment)
7. NORTH (Queen's seat)
8. FLIRT (Pudding)
9. MEETS (Units of length)
10. RETAIN (Sure)

If two's company, and three's a crowd, what's four and five?

91: BURIED ANIMALS

Can you spot the well-known animals and birds hidden somewhere in these sentences?

1. You have been invited to a dance on Friday.
2. I would rather play cricket than watch it.
3. Jane's hairdo goes with her outfit.
4. Because he is a vegetarian, Peter abhors every kind of meat.
5. When I saw the tramp, I gave him my last apple.
6. Now, let me see what I can do.
7. She still felt a throb in her arm many days later.
8. The shop did not have the particular kind of clothes I liked.
9. I could see a gleam in her eye.
10. This transmitter can send out micro-waves.

Mr Pugh did not believe in wasting anything. He even kept all his old cigarette butts so that he could use them to make new cigarettes! Mr Pugh bought exactly five cigarettes a day, and from every five butts he collected, he was able to make one whole new cigarette, which he then also smoked. Can you work out how many cigarettes Mr Pugh would smoke in five days?

93: CLEVER LETTERS

You would never have thought it, but letters can be very clever indeed! Can you tell me which two letters of the alphabet can be 'said' to sound like the following?

a. COLD   **e.** AN ENGLISH COUNTY
b. A GIRL'S NAME **f.** A RED INDIAN TENT
c. VACANT   **g.** A NUMBER
d. JEALOUSY   **h.** TO ROT

94: IT'S ALL THE SAME

Can you find an amazing similarity between the numbers 10 and 11?

95: KNOW YOUR TREES

How well do you know the names for all the different kinds of trees? If you do, here is a chance to match the tree to the clue. What tree:

a. Has been burnt?
b. Is found in bottles?
c. Is by the sea?
d. Is a couple?
e. Is a punishment?
f. Longs for something?
g. Is in our hands?
h. Cries a lot?
i. Warms you up?
j. Is liked by everyone?

96: AT FIVES AND SEVENS

If a certain number is reduced by seven, and multiplied by seven, it will give the same answer as if it were reduced by five, and multiplied by five. Do you know what the number is?

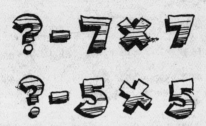

97: DON'T BELIEVE YOUR EYES

Have a good look at this diagram, and tell me whether you think the gap between A and B is more or less than the gap between C and B.

98: VERY ODD

Can you think of five odd numbers which, added together, make fourteen?

99: WORD PHRASE

Have a guess at what phrase the word below represents. Here is a clue — it is all too common in this country!

WETHER

100: A MAN AND A CAR

Here is one which will really stretch your mind.

A man pushed his car up to a hotel, and realised that he had lost all his money.

Can you supply the missing links in this sad story? One clue: The car has not run out of petrol, and has not broken down. . .

101: PUSSIES GALORE

Susie Simpkin owned a number of cats. All but two of them were black, all but two of them were tabby, and all but two of them were ginger. How many cats did Susie own?

William Brown met Clarence at the bus-stop.

"Don't I know you?" enquired William.

"You should do," replied Clarence. "Your father was my father's only son."

How are they related?

103: LOST BOTTLES

Billy Bottle, the milkman, worked out that each month he lost 10 per cent (to the nearest unit) of his bottles, through breakages, bottles not being returned, and so on. If he started on 1 January with 1000 bottles, and did not replace any losses, how many bottles would he have left on 31 December?

104: MIRRORED TIME

If you see the reflection of a clock in a mirror and the time appears to be 2.30, what time is it really?

105: PUZZLE PICTURE

Take a look at this drawing. What is it?

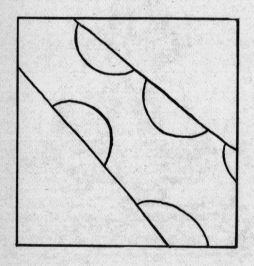

106: FOUR-MIDDABLE!

Here is a puzzle for geniuses only! Can you find the four-digit number in which:

a. The last digit is twice the first.
b. The second digit is twice the third.
c. The sum of the first and last digits is twice the second.

107: FARMER'S PROBLEM

Farmer Gyles's sheep and goats have got muddled up. Here they are, and each sheep is next to a goat:

Can you, in three moves only, and moving only the neighbouring animals, end up with all the sheep together and all the goats together, as shown below?

Arnold Columbus was a great traveller. He had visited most parts of the world at least once, and on his trunk were labels showing the names of some of the countries he had been to. Unfortunately Arnold had a very naughty young son called Albert, who, one April Fool's Day, cut each label up into little pieces and stuck the letters back on the trunk in the wrong order. This is what Arnold saw when he looked at it on the morning of 1 April. Can you work out which countries the labels spell out?

1. A N A L O G
2. R A I N
3. L A I T Y
4. S E R I A L
5. I N L A C E D
6. P U R E
7. C H A I N
8. R E G A L I A
9. E N G L A N D E R
10. P L A N E

109: NEW CLOTHES

A pair of trousers and a belt cost £21. The trousers cost £20 more than the belt. What was the price of each?

110: FACT AND FICTION

Can you tell fact from fiction? Some of these statements are true, and some are false. Can you spot which is which?

1. A glockenspiel is a musical instrument.
2. A gargoyle is a kind of mouthwash.
3. There are more black squares than white squares on a chessboard.
4. A Chihuahua is a breed of dog.
5. If you have acute nasopharyngitis it isn't serious, you just have a cold.
6. The capital of Greenland is Reykjavik.
7. Liechtenstein is the smallest country in Europe.
8. Cows have four stomachs.

111: EX-STRAW-DINARY!

Set out six straws like this:

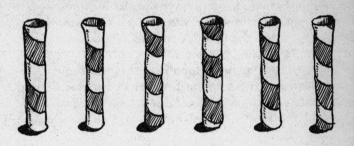

Now see if you can add five more straws to make nine!

112: CAT WORDS

Can you think of a word beginning with CAT to fit each of the following meanings:

1. Disaster
2. A twin-hulled boat
3. A list
4. A device for shooting missiles
5. A flower that grows on a tree in spring
6. A class, or division, in a classification

113: SAVINGS BANK

Have you ever tried to save up for your holidays, or for Christmas, only to discover at the end of your period of saving that you haven't got nearly as much money as you thought you would have? If so, try doing it this way. Start on the first day of a new month.

On the first of the month, save 1p.

On the second of the month, save twice as much, 2p.

On the third of the month, save twice as much again, 4p.

On the fourth of the month, save twice as much again, 8p.

Keep doing this throughout the month, on each day saving twice as much as you did before. If you do this, and the month has 31 days, how much money will you have saved by the end of it?

114: SUM PUZZLE

Here's another mathematical puzzle. Can this addition sum possibly be right?

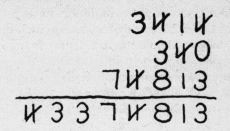

115: DOZENS OUT

What's the difference between six dozen dozen and half a dozen dozen?

116: WORD LADDERS

Do you know what a word ladder is? It's a way of changing one word to another by changing just one letter at a time. For example, you can change CAT to DOG in three moves:
CAT
COT
DOT
DOG
Now see if you can change GIVE to TAKE in four moves.

117: HIDDEN GIRLS

Hidden in each of these sentences is a girl's name. How many can you spot?

1. ''Can Neville come out and play now?''
2. ''I said no rabbits were to come in the house!''
3. The valley was covered in a white haze, lying low over the land.
4. ''Did you see the heath, Ernie?''
5. The jewel was kept wrapped in a hanky.
6. Leaning on the bar, Barabbas spoke.
7. ''Would you like a pear, Lionel?''
8. He drove the dodgem, making everyone scream.
9. ''Pull down the blind,'' says Mother.
10. ''Did Ma bellow at you when you were late?''

118: CHANGE THE SHAPE

Here's a puzzle you can work out for yourself if you have a pencil, a ruler, some paper and a pair of scissors. Look at the rectangle below. Can you cut it into five parts to form a perfect square?

119: WHAT'S NEXT?

What is the next number in each of the series below?

2	3	5	9	17	33
31	28	31	30		

120: THE LAST STRAW

Set out twelve straws like this:
1. Now see if you can move four straws and leave two squares.
2. Remove two straws and leave two squares.
3. Move two straws and make seven squares.

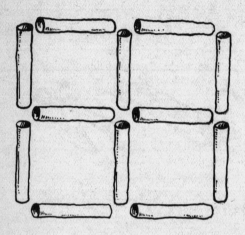

121: PRESENT MUDDLE

Grandma Wilkinson was very fond of her three grand-children, Betty, Billy and Ben. Each child had a pet that he or she loved very much, and Grandma Wilkinson tried each Christmas to give the children presents relating to their pets. The trouble was, she could never remember which pet was which, nor who owned them! She was only sure of five things:

1. That Simon was a cat.
2. That Betty did not own a dog
3. That the donkey's owner was not Billy.
4. That Susie's owner was Ben.
5. That Sam was a dog.

Knowing these facts, can you work out what each pet was called, and to whom it belonged?

122: SPELLING BEE

How good is your spelling? In each of these lists of words only one is spelt correctly. Can you spot which one it is and correct the other two?

1. Parrafin, parallel, parrakeet.
2. Stony, grimey, prettie.
3. Gaurding, gluing, growning.
4. Alsation, Doberman, Pekingese.
5. Flourescent, weird, counterfeit.
6. Desiccated, decimmated, dellineated.
7. Excercise, rythm, waltz.
8. Addvertise, parallyse, synchronise.
9. Necessary, mantlepiece, predjudice.
10. Sphagetti, pizza, raviolli.

123: DOUBLE DUTCH

This message is not written in a foreign language, but in English. Can you work out what it says?

A NYON EWH OC ANRE ADT HISMES SAGEI NTE NSECO NDSIS AGE NIUS.

124: WHEELING AND DEALING

An antiques dealer sold a chair for £35 and half as much as he had paid for it a few weeks before. His profit was £10.50. How much did he pay for the chair?

125: WORD SOUNDS

In English there are lots of words that sound the same but which are spelt differently and which have completely different meanings, for example, YOU, the pronoun, and EWE, a female sheep. Can you find ten pairs of words that sound the same to match the definitions below?

1. To chop wood/colour.
2. A kind of leather/moved to and fro.
3. A sphere/to cry loudly.
4. A domestic servant/created.
5. A wild cat/parts of a chain.
6. A swordfight/double.
7. Rough/the route to follow.
8. Breaking the rules in football/a chicken.
9. To pick/what someone does with food in the mouth.
10. A climb/agreement.

126: DESPERATE MEASURES

Bertha Baggins was a keen young cook who always measured all the ingredients in her dishes very precisely. One day she was busy making lemonade and her recipe said to add a pint of water. But all she could find in her kitchen was a three-pint jug and a five-pint jug. How could she measure the water? (She didn't have a milk bottle, either!)

127: A QUESTION OF COLOUR

Hank McDiggle was an old trapper who lived in the backwoods of Canada. He kept his clothes thrown together in an old trunk and whenever he went into town people would laugh at him because his socks were different colours. This was because Hank put them on in the dark. Hank had 36 socks altogether – eighteen of them brown ones and eighteen of them green ones. How many socks must he take out of the trunk to make sure of having one matching pair? And how many would he have to take out to be sure of having six matching pairs?

128: LETTER RACK

What comes next in these sequences of letters?

1. A C F J O
2. Z W S P L
3. S M T W

129: RIDDLE-ME-REE

Here are some mindstretching riddles. Can you solve them all?

1. What is always coming but never arrives?
2. What is full of holes but holds water?
3. What is very light, yet impossible to hold for more than a few seconds?
4. What is bought by the metre and worn by the foot?
5. What lives on itself, but dies as soon as it has used up all of itself?

130: A MATTER OF TIMING

Minnie Minute has two clocks. The older clock has stopped and will never work again. The newer clock gains half a minute every twenty-four hours. Which clock tells the correct time more often?

There is only one NEEDLE hidden in this square haystack. Can you find it?

```
E L D E N E E D E L N E E N E D L
L E E N E D L E N E E D E L N E E
D E E L E N D L E E D E N E E D L
E D N E L E E N E L E E L E E N E
N E E L D E E D N L E D E N D E N
E N L E E D E L E D E E N E L E L
E E D E N N E E L E D L E N D E E
D E D E L E E D N E E L D E L L D
N L E N E L D L E N E E L D N E E
E D E D L N E E E D L E N E E D L
L E L D E L N E L E N E D E D N E
N E E D N E D E D E E D E N L E L
N E L D E E E E L N E E L E D E E
N E D E L D E N E E D L N E E L D
E N D E E L E N E N E E L D E E E
E L E N N E E E D L E N E E L N N
E E D L E N E L E N E L E N E N D
```

132: ZOO TIME

Can you complete these three words? In each one the missing letters spell out the name of an animal.

a. P Y - - - I D
b. B R - - - R Y
c. E D U - - - I O N

133: MORE ANIMALS

Can you think of a creature that lives in water whose name begins with two EEs? And can you think of a creature that lives on land whose name begins with two LLs?

134: MARTIAN ARTS

A to I are nine positions in a ring of Martian soldiers who are practising a deadly game. They are standing facing inwards, and the idea of the game is that, starting with the General at A, each Martian destroys the man on his immediate left with his deadly ray-gun, until only one Martian is left. If the game was played for real, which Martian would survive?

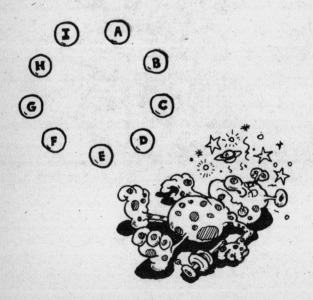

The sentences below each have a number of letters missing from them. If they look vaguely familiar to you, it is because they are all well-known English proverbs.

a. A S T T C H N T M E S A V E S N N E
b. T M A N Y C K S S P I L T H E B R T H
c. A R L L I N G T O N E G A T H E R N O - M O
d. A B I R D I T H E H N D I S W O R H W - O I N H E B U S H
e. M N Y H N D S M K E L I G H T W O R K
f. M I S S I S S G O O D S M I L E

g. T H A R L Y B I R D C A T C H S T H W-
O R M

h. N V E R L K A G I F T H R S E I N T H E-
M U T H

i. O O K B E F O R E Y O U E A P

j. R L T B D R L T R S M K S M N H L T H-
W L T H N D W S

136: FRUIT BASKET

Can you take the word LUMP and turn it into a fruit?
And can you take the word LEMON and turn it into
another fruit?

137: LETTERS SEE

Here are five rows of letters. One row doesn't belong to the series. Can you spot which it is?

I C A B
I C A C
I C A J
I C A U
I C A Z

138: ON THE BUSES

At High Fell on the Hill there is a local bus service that runs between the railway station (at the bottom of the hill) and the town (at the top). The journey takes ten minutes in each direction and the buses wait for five minutes at the station on each trip. One afternoon at 2 pm, bus number 212 is driving along and due to reach the station at 2.15. When will it pass the bus ahead of it, number 211?

139: SHAPING UP

Which two shapes in this circle are the same?

140: HOT STUFF

What burns no coal, no oil, no wood, no gas, uses no electricity, yet is far hotter than all the ovens and fires and blast furnaces in the world?

141: COINING IT?

Arrange seven coins in a letter H shape as shown below.

If you count the diagonal lines, as well as the vertical and horizontal ones, you will see there are five rows with three coins in a row. Now add an extra two coins to the pattern to make a new pattern which incorporates ten rows with three coins in each row.

THE ANSWERS

1. Emma: Brown. Sally: Orange. Richard: White. Alison: Blue.

2. Because it would be the middle of the night again!

3.

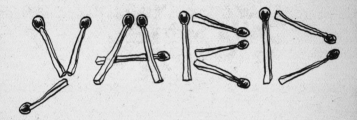

4. She read the number 86 upside down.

5. He gave his fifth daughter her egg *in* the basket.

6. Only one weighing. This is how it is done. Take one coin from the first stack, two from the second, three from the third, and so on, up to ten from the tenth stack. Now weigh all these coins (55) on the scale. Any excess weight above 550 grams (55 times 10) must be due to the forgeries, and the number of grams above 550 is exactly the number of the stack which contains those forgeries.

7. DENY. DREAMT.

8. 15 weeks.

9. Seven.

10. Place three in a 'triangle', and balance the fourth on top.

11. Four — I did say it was a small room!

12. There are two ways of doing it:

a.

b.

13. The water will never cover the rung. As the water rises, so does the rope ladder!

14. They could not have known that Christ was going to be born back in 55 BC!

15. They were both at exactly the same distance from London.

16. 1961.

17. 23.

18. £2.

19. 100 kilos of gold is always worth more than 50 kilos of gold, whatever each individual bar is worth.

20. A wolf does not eat corn, so he takes the hen over first, leaving it on the other side. He then takes the corn over. On the other side, he leaves the corn, but takes the hen back with him. He then leaves the hen on the first bank, and takes the wolf across. He leaves the corn with the wolf, and rows back to the first bank alone. Finally he takes the hen across.

21. Water. HIJKLMNO is H to O, or H_2O which is the chemical sign for water.

22. Four brothers and three sisters.

23. $888 + 88 + 8 + 8 + 8 = 1000$.

24. $111 - 11 = 100$.

25. 140 in all!

26. 1½.

27. **a.** 44 **b.** 18 **c.** 31 **d.** 16 **e.** 53.

28. 400 earrings. Among the 95 per cent, if half wear two earrings and half none, it's the same as if each wore one.

29. Neither. Yolks are yellow!

30. 11 seconds.

31. Joan, where Hazel had 'had', had 'had had'. 'Had had' had had the teacher's approval.

32. One hour 20 minutes is the same as 80 minutes!
33. She had sugared her original cup of coffee.

34. **1.** Elephant **2.** Alligator **3.** Rattlesnake **4.** Orangutan **5.** Water Buffalo.

35. He said, *"The spaces between 'Fish' and 'and' and 'and' and 'Chips' are too big."*

36. £13, 212.

37. The parrot was deaf!

38. The answer is 0.

39. **b.** and **d.** are wrong, so there are only two sums which are wrong — that is the third mistake!

40. Since there were only two barbers in the town, each must have cut the other's hair. The cowboy picked the barber who had given his rival the better haircut.

41. Five apples!

42. Nil. If three letters go into the right envelopes, so will the fourth.

43. Five minutes.

44. Midnight on Saturday.

45. 909.

46. a. The Seven Seas **b.** I understand you **c.** Not before time (No — t before time!) **d.** Girl overslept **e.** In between times.

47. They went and stood one either side of a large Bank!

48. If each man at a circular table is either a 'truther' or a 'liar', and each man says that the man on his left is a 'liar', there must be an even number of people at the table, arranged so that 'truthers' and 'liars' are sitting next to each other. The President must have been lying when he said there were 35 men present. Since the Secretary called the President a 'liar', he must be a 'truther' — therefore he spoke the truth when he gave the number present as 40.

49. Adding the bellboy's £2 to the £17 Freddy paid for the room produces a meaningless sum. Freddy has parted with £17, of which the clerk has £15 and the bellboy £2. Freddy got back £3, which, added to the £17 held by the clerk and bellboy, makes up the full £20.

50.

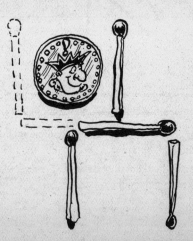

51. O — that is why it is called a hole!

52. **a.** Tom Tom **b.** Beneath **c.** Jackpot **d.** Pathetic **e.** Marketable **f.** Philosopher **g.** Leopard.

53. Seventy-three. There was no year 0.

54. 50p and 5p. One of the coins was not a 50-pence piece, but the other one was!

55. £1. There were only three men in all — a grandfather, a father, and a son.

56. Some would say £7, because the the tobacconist got £5 and the man £2. In fact, the owner of the sweet shop only lost £5 to the tobacconist.

57. The mule had seven, the donkey five.

58.

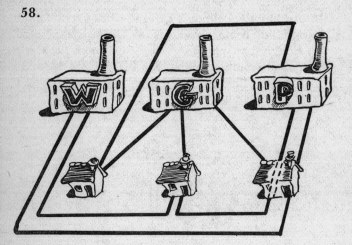

59. First add the parts given as fractions:

$$\frac{1}{6} + \frac{1}{12} + \frac{1}{7} + \frac{1}{2} = \frac{14 + 7 + 12 + 42}{84} = \frac{75}{84}$$

$\frac{9}{84}$ of his life is not accounted for. We are told, however, of two other periods — one of four years, the other of five (a total of nine years). This means that $\frac{1}{84}$ of his life is one year. So the answer is that Diophantes lived to be 84.

60. Neither way — it is an electric train!

61. The answer seems to be 3 piastres for the first shepherd, and 5 for the second, but it is not. After dividing 8 loaves between the three of them, each had 2⅔ loaves. If the hunter paid 8 piastres for 2⅔ loaves, it follows that 8 loaves cost 24 piastres, and one loaf costs 3 piastres. The first shepherd, who started with 3 loaves and ended up with 2⅔, only gave the hunter ⅓ loaf; the second shepherd, who started with 5 loaves and ended up with 2⅔, gave the hunter 2⅓ loaves. Therefore, 1 piastre goes to the first shepherd, and 7 to the second.

62. Two worms in love!

63. a. 5, 21. **b.** 3, 2. **c.** 384, 512. **d.** 5 (It is the number of letters in the words from one to eight). **e.** 9 (It is the number of hours sleep I got last week!)

64. Three and a half minutes — if they are all done at the same time.

65. CODE BREAKERS OF THE WORLD UNITE. Each number corresponds to the letter's position in the alphabet.

66. Yes. One is black, and the other is white!

67. 1. IAN 2. TOM 3. ERIC 4. ALAN 5. LEN
6. TIM 7. RAY 8. CARL 9. SAM 10. ROY.

68.

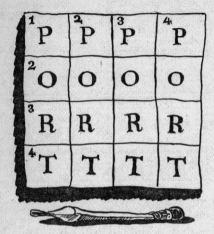

69. Yes, but only if they are not pushed through at the same time!

70. John.

71. 14 triangles.

72. IT'S NOT EASY WHEN LETTERS SLIP AND SLIDE.

73.

74.

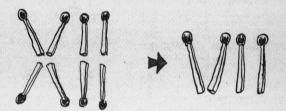

75. 300 kilometres.

76. UNDERGROUND.

77. Starting at point E, follow this route: E-B-D-C-B-A-C-F-D-E-F.

78. Starting at point C, follow this route: C-D-J-F-H-J-K-E-F-B-E-A-C-F.

79.

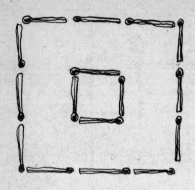

80.

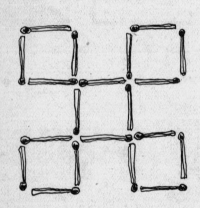

81. 1. Abomination **2.** Assassination **3.** Imperson-
ation **4.** Examination **5.** Illumination **6.** Carn-
ation **7.** Fascination **8.** Destination **9.** Imagination **10.** Termination.

82. One.

83. 1. SAUSAGE 2. SCRUMMAGE
3. VOLTAGE 4. POSTAGE 5. BAGGAGE
6. BEVERAGE 7. PLUMAGE.

84. The horizontal line.

85. The ten of diamonds, the king of hearts, and the eight of spades.

86. Light the match first, of course!

87. a. Ham b. Currants c. Corn d. Jam e. Leeks
f. Soles g. Steaks h. Lettuce alone!

88. AB and CD are exactly the same distance.

89. 1. Silent 2. Beach 3. Butler 4. Chums 5. Planet
6. Shirt 7. Throne 8. Trifle 9. Metres 10. Certain.

90. NINE!

91. 1. TOAD 2. RAT 3. DOG 4. HORSE 5. PIG
6. OWL 7. ROBIN 8. LARK 9. EAGLE
10. CROW.

92. 31.

93. a. I-C b. K-T c. M-T d. N-V e. S-X f. T-P
g. A-T h. D-K.

94. Two times ten is twenty, and two times eleven is twenty too!

95. a. Ash b. Cork c. Beech d. Pear e. Birch f. Pine
g. Palm h. Weeping Willow i. Fir j. Poplar.

96. 12.

97. The gaps between A and B, and B and C are exactly the same.

98. $11 + 1 + 1 + 1 = 14$.

99. A bad spell of weather!

100. The man is playing a game of Monopoly! His car has landed on a property with a hotel on it, and he has had to pay a hefty rent.

101. Three cats: one black, one tabby and one ginger.

102. Clarence is William's father.

103. 282. In January he loses 10% of 1000: 1000 − 100 = 900; in February he loses 10% of 900: 900 − 90 = 810; in March he loses 10% of 810: 810 − 81 = 729; in April he loses 10% of 729: 729 − 73 = 656; in May he loses 10% of 656: 656 − 66 = 590; in June he loses 10% of 590: 590 − 59 = 531; in July he loses 10% of 531: 531 − 53 = 478; in August he loses 10% of 478: 478 − 48 = 430; in September he loses 10% of 430: 430 − 43 = 387; in October he loses 10% of 387: 387 − 39 = 348; in November he loses 10% of 348: 348 − 35 = 313; in December he loses 10% of 313: 313 − 31 = 282.

104. 9.30.

105. A giraffe walking past a second-storey window!

106. 4638.

107. First move: sheep, goat, sheep, goat, goat, sheep.
Second move: sheep, sheep, goat, goat, goat, sheep.
Third move: sheep, sheep, sheep, goat, goat, goat.

108. 1. ANGOLA   **2.** IRAN   **3.** ITALY
4. ISRAEL   **5.** ICELAND   **6.** PERU
7. CHINA **8.** ALGERIA **9.** GREENLAND
10. NEPAL

109. The trousers cost £20.50 and the belt 50p.

110. 1. True **2.** False **3.** False **4.** True **5.** True
6. False **7.** False **8.** True

111.

112. 1. CATastrophe **2.** CATamaran
 3. CATalogue **4.** CATapult **5.** CATkin
 6. CATegory

113. £21,474,834!

114. Try looking at it through a mirror!

115. Six dozen dozen is 864, half a dozen dozen is 72.
 The difference is 792.

116. GIVE; LIVE; LIKE; LAKE; TAKE.

117. 1. Anne **2.** Nora **3.** Hazel **4.** Heather
 5. Dinah **6.** Barbara **7.** Pearl **8.** Gemma
 9. Lindsay **10.** Mabel.

118. This is how it's done.

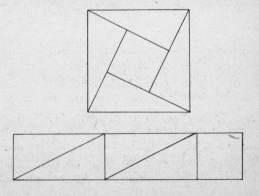

119. 65 - each number is double the previous number minus 1.

31 - they are the number of days in the month starting with January.

120.

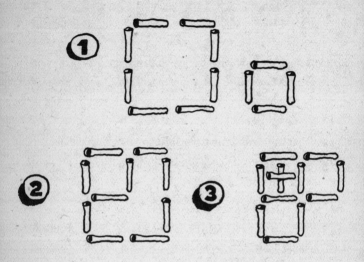

121. Simon, the cat, belonged to Betty. Sam, the dog, belonged to Billy. Susie, the donkey, belonged to Ben.

122. **1.** Parallel is correct, the others should be paraffin and parakeet. **2.** Stony is correct, the others should be grimy and pretty. **3.** Gluing is correct, the others should be guarding and groaning. **4.** Pekingese is correct, the others should be Alsatian and Dobermann. **5.** Weird is correct, the others should be fluorescent and counterfeit. **6.** Desiccated is correct, the others should be decimated and delineated. **7.** Waltz is correct, the others should be exercise and rhythm. **8.** Synchronise is correct, the others should be advertise and paralyse. **9.** Necessary is correct, the others should be mantelpiece and prejudice. **10.** Pizza is correct, the others should be spaghetti and ravioli.

123. ANYONE WHO CAN READ THIS MESSAGE IN TEN SECONDS IS A GENIUS.

124. £49.

125. **1.** Hew/hue **2.** Suede/swayed **3.** Ball/bawl **4.** Maid/made **5.** Lynx/links **6.** Duel/dual **7.** Coarse/course **8.** Foul/fowl **9.** Choose/chews **10.** Ascent/assent.

126. First, she should fill the three-pint jug, and empty it into the five-pint jug. Then she should refill the three-pint jug and pour as much of the water as will go into the five-pint jug. What remains in the three-pint jug will then be exactly one pint.

127. Three. Thirteen.

128. **1.** U. The sequence goes through the alphabet missing out first one letter, then two, then three, then four, then five, then six. **2.** I E B. This time the sequence goes backwards, missing out two letters, then three, then two, then three, and so on. **3.** T F S. They are the first letters of the days of the week.

129. **1.** Tomorrow **2.** A sponge **3.** Your breath **4.** A carpet **5.** A candle.

130. The older clock is correct twice every day, but the newer clock is only correct every 720 days.

```
E L D E N E E D E L N E E N E D L
L E E N E D L E N E E D E L N E E
D E E L E N D L E E D E N E E D L
E D N E L E E N E L E E L E E N E
N E E L D E E D N L E D E N D E N
E N L E E D E L E D E E N E L E L
E E D E N N E E L E D L E N D E E
D E D E L E E D N E E L D E L L D
N L E N E L D L E N E E L D N E E
E D E D L N E E E D L E N E E D L
L E L D E L N E L E N E D E D N E
N E E D N E D E D E E D E N L E L
N E L D E E E E L N E E L E D E E
N E D E L D E N E E D L N E E L D
E N D E E L E N E N E E L D E E E
E L E N N E E D L E N E E L N N
E E D L E N E L E N E L E N E N D
```

132. a. P Y R A M I D **b.** B R E W E R Y
c. E D U C A T I O N

133. Eel; llama.

134. C would survive. A would destroy B, C would
destroy D, E would destroy F, G would destroy
H, I would destroy A. On the next round, C
would destroy E, and G would destroy I. Finally,
C would destroy G.

135. a. I is missing. The sentence should read: A STITCH IN TIME SAVES NINE. **b.** O is missing. The sentence should read: TOO MANY COOKS SPOIL THE BROTH. **c.** An O is missing and several Ss. The sentence should read: A ROLLING STONE GATHERS NO MOSS.

d. An N, an A and three Ts are missing. The sentence should read: A BIRD IN THE HAND IS WORTH TWO IN THE BUSH. **e.** A is missing. The sentence should read: MANY HANDS MAKE LIGHT WORK. **f.** A is missing again. The sentence should read: A MISS IS AS GOOD AS A MILE. **g.** E is missing. The sentence should read: THE EARLY BIRD CATCHES THE WORM. **h.** An E and several Os are missing. The sentence should read: NEVER LOOK A GIFT HORSE IN THE MOUTH. **i.** L is missing. The sentence should read: LOOK BEFORE YOU LEAP. **j.** A, E, I, O, U and Y are missing. The sentence should read: EARLY TO BED, EARLY TO RISE, MAKES A MAN HEALTHY, WEALTHY AND WISE.

136. PLUM; MELON.

137. ICAZ is the odd man out. All the other letters can be read as sentences that make sense, e.g. I see a bee, I see a sea.

138. At 2.12½. Bus no. 211 will reach the station at 2.05. After five minutes it will start back up the hill, at 2.10. Bus no. 212 will then be five minutes away from the station. So they should meet halfway, two and a half minutes later, at 2.12½.

139. Nos. 2 and 7.

140. The sun.

141.

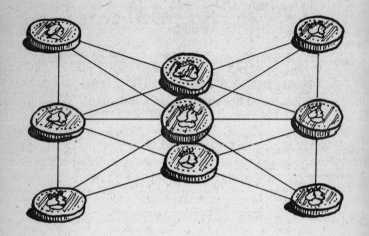

THE BIG BOOK OF GHASTLY RHYMES
by Gyles Brandreth

> Bessie met a bus,
> The bus met Bessie,
> The bus was messy,
> The mess was Bessie.

> Willie, with a thirst for gore,
> Nailed his sister to the door.
> Mother said, with humour quaint:
> "Willie dear, don't scratch the paint!"

Awful odes, rude and ridiculous rhymes, ludicrous lime-ricks, vile verse and worse. All here in THE BIG BOOK OF GHASTLY RHYMES – poetry to make you groan as well as giggle!

0 552 54273 3   £1.50

THE BIG BOOK OF SILLY QUESTIONS
by Gyles Brandreth

* If 'Dr. Livingstone, I presume,' was the answer, what was the question?
  'What is your full name, Dr. Presume?'
* Which is bigger, Mrs Bigger or Mrs Bigger's baby?
  Mrs Bigger's baby is a little Bigger!'
* Which is colder, −40°C or −40°F?
  They are both the same!

If you think these questions are silly – wait until you see the rest of the book. And some of the ridiculous quizzes are not as crazy as they may seem . . .

0 552 54263 6   £1.50

1000 WORD WONDERS
by Gyles Brandreth

DAFT DEFINITION: *Robin: a bird that steals*

HOWLER: *Noah's wife was Joan of Arc*

PUN: *Is a sourpuss a cat that has swallowed a lemon?*

WORD PICTURE: M   E
                  A   L   = *a square meal*

Spoonersims, riddles, tongue-twisters, and 996 more fascinating WORD WONDERS that are guaranteed to keep you amused and amazed for hours . . .

0 552 54266 0   £1.50

1000 BRAIN-TEASERS: MIND-BOGGLERS TO BOGGLE YOUR MIND

by Gyles Brandreth

*Which is faster, hot or cold?
*Where does a fisherman keep his LOOPS of line?
*Can you think of a word with motion which added to both 'up' and 'down' has the same meaning in both cases?

And there are 997 more to do! With hundreds to choose from, there's a brainteaser for everyone. There are picture puzzles, tricky word puzzles, puzzles and questions about figures for those of you with calculator brains – and plenty of puzzles that only need a quick mind and a bit of imagination. On with your thinking caps and happy puzzling!

0 552 54257 1   £1.50

SHOWTIME
by Brian Cant

Have you ever longed to put on your own show, act out a play, entertain your family and friends with magic tricks or comedy sketches?

Actor Brian Cant shows you how to:
  Transform any room into a theatre
  Make finger and hand puppets
  Make 'A Pin to see the Peepshow'
  Make a model theatre
  Create your own sound effects
  Make hand shadows
  Perform magic tricks

With scripts and sketches to act out, tips on costume and make-up, and lots of ideas to amaze and amuse, excite and delight – it's SHOWTIME!

0 552 54268 7   £1.50

If you would like to receive a Newsletter about our new Children's books, just fill in the coupon below with your name and address (or copy it onto a separate piece of paper if you don't want to spoil your book) and send it to:

The Children's Books Editor
Young Corgi Books
61–63 Uxbridge Road,
Ealing
London W5 5SA

Please send me a Children's Newsletter:

Name . . . .

Address . . . .

. . . .

. . . .

All the books on the previous pages are available at your local bookshop or can be ordered direct from the publishers: Cash Sales Dept., Transworld Publishers Ltd., 61–63 Uxbridge Road, Ealing, London W5 5SA.

Please enclose the cost of the book(s), together with the following for postage and packing costs:

Orders up to a value of £5.00   50p
Orders of a value over £5.00   Free

Please note that payment should be made by cheque or postal order in £ sterling.